# Sally Goes to the Vet

## Written and Illustrated by
## Stephen Huneck

Harry N. Abrams, Inc., Publishers

## ARTIST'S NOTE

This book is special to me as I am so appreciative of the loving care veterinarians give our animal companions. They are with us at our happiest moments, when we are told our best friend is going to be okay, but also at our saddest, when we have to say good-bye. By their dedication they show us that the fellow creatures we share this planet with all have great dignity and worth.

To create a woodcut print, I first draw the design of the future print in crayon, laying out the prospective shapes and colors. I then carve one block of wood for each color in the appropriate shape. The result is a series of carved blocks, one for each color in the print. After a block has been inked with its respective color, acid-free archival paper is laid onto the block and hand rubbed. I repeat the process for each color block. When this process is completed, I hang the prints to dry.

I wish to thank all the talented people at Harry N. Abrams, Inc., especially my editor, Howard Reeves. My thanks to Mike Lamp for his dedication to Dog Mountain, and to Pam Wasserman for her tremendous enthusiasm. To my wife, Gwen, who contributes so much to my life and work, I can't thank you enough. And to one very special vet, Dr. Gus Aguirre, my thanks.

www.huneck.com

Library of Congress Cataloging-in-Publication Data

Huneck, Stephen.

Sally goes to the vet / written and illustrated by Stephen Huneck.
p. cm.
Summary: Sally the dog goes flying over a tree stump while playing chase in the yard and has to be rushed to the vet's office.
ISBN 0-8109-4813-3
[1. Dogs—Fiction. 2. Veterinarians—Fiction.] I. Title.

PZ7.H8995Sap 2004
[E]—dc22
2003019911

Text and illustrations copyright © 2004 Stephen Huneck

Published in 2004 by Harry N. Abrams, Incorporated, New York.

Printed and bound in China
10 9 8 7 6 5 4 3 2 1

Harry N. Abrams, Inc.
100 Fifth Avenue
New York, NY 10011
www.abramsbooks.com

Abrams is a subsidiary of

LA MARTINIÈRE
GROUPE

Stephen
Huneck

To vets everywhere—thank you!

It has been raining for days.

I have been stuck inside with nothing to do.

At last, the sun is shining.
I can go outside and play!

I find my friend Bingo in a tree.
We like to play the chasing game.

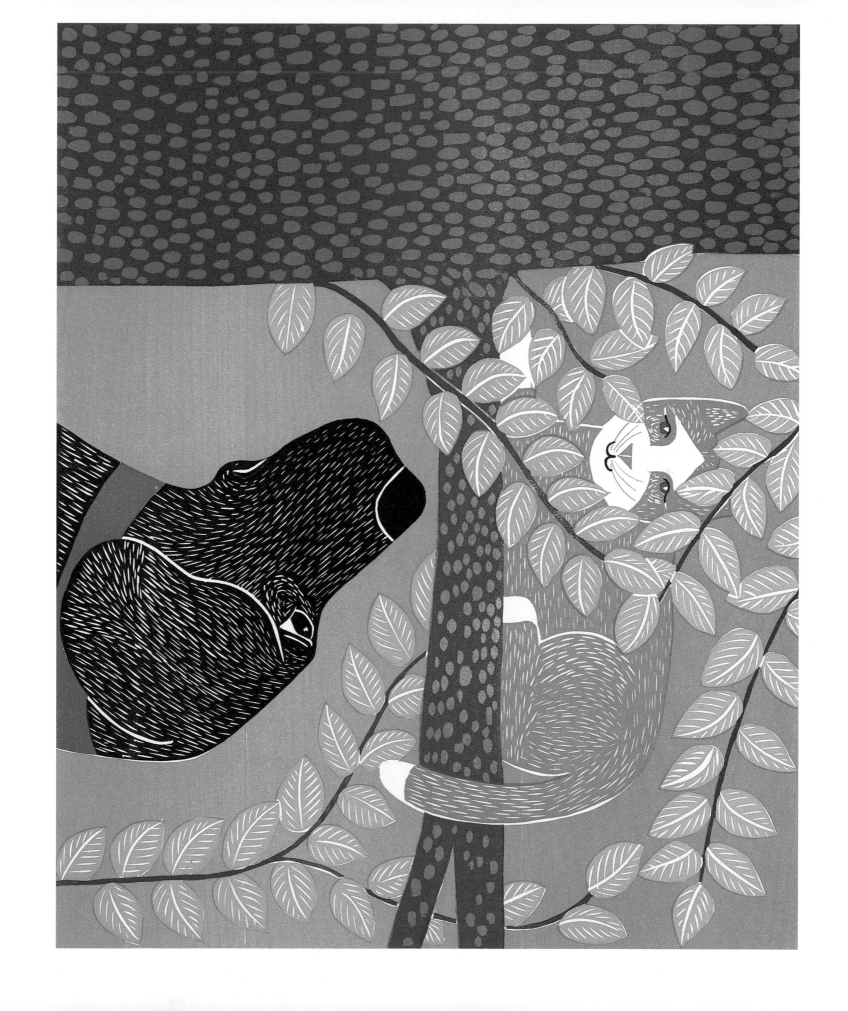

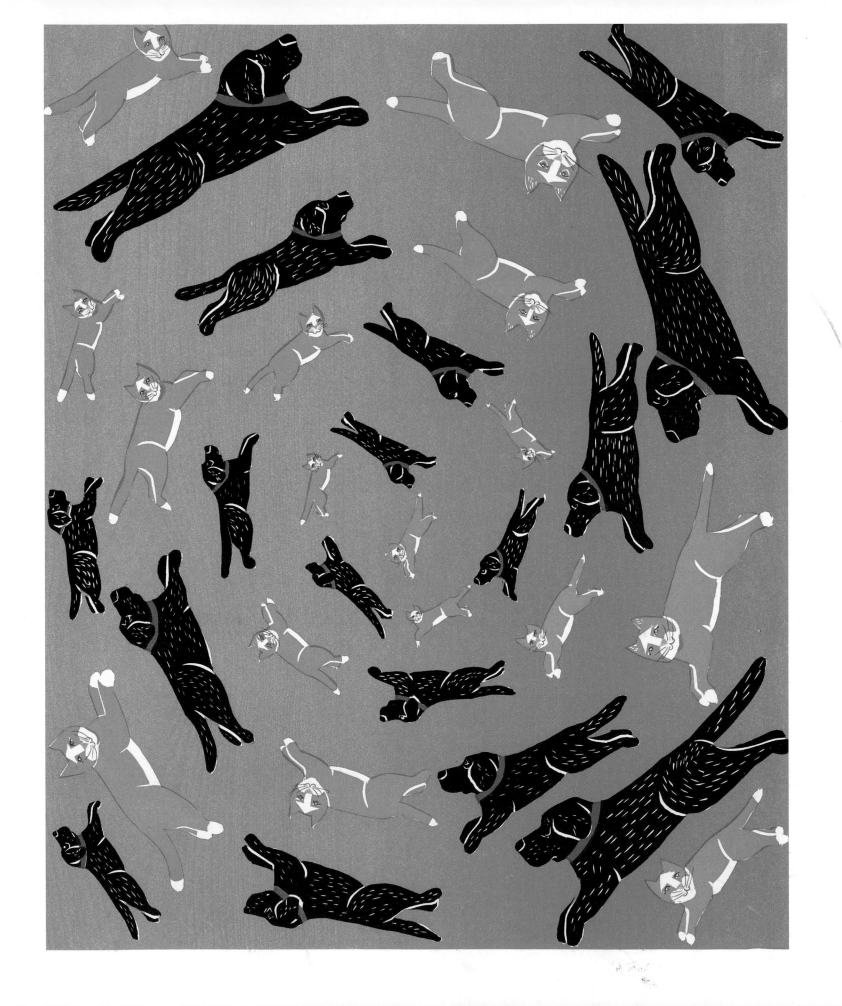

First I chase Bingo.

Then Bingo chases me.

I am running so fast,
I do not see the tree stump.

I go flying
through the air . . . .

and land with a ground-shaking thump!

I hear someone say,
"Sally is hurt! Quick,
take her to the vet."

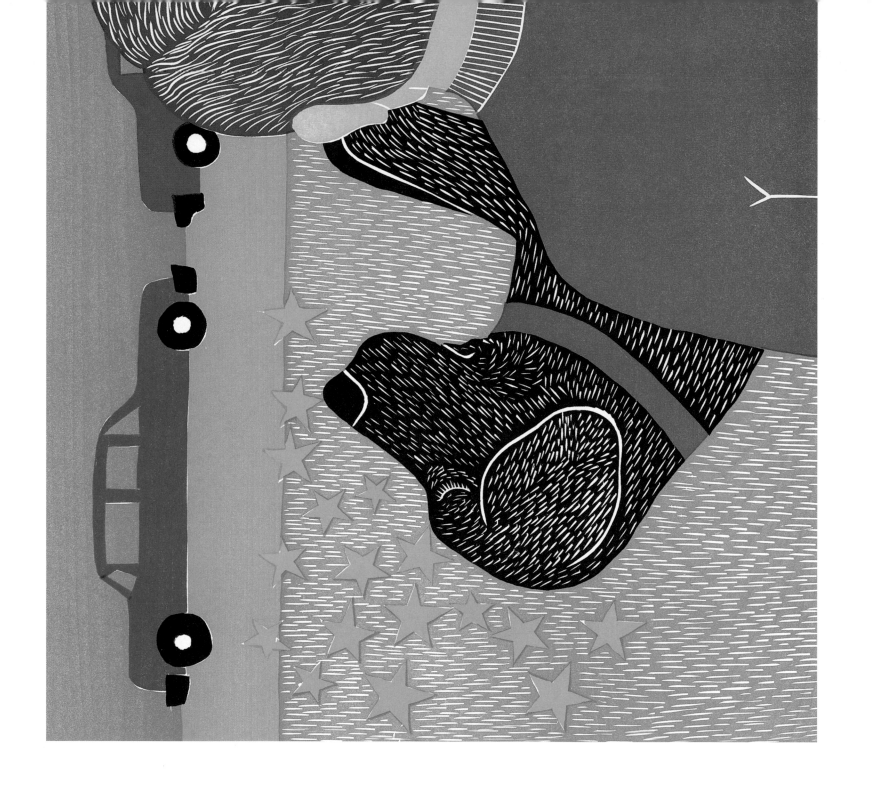

I am carried to the car. I lie down in

back all the way to the animal hospital.

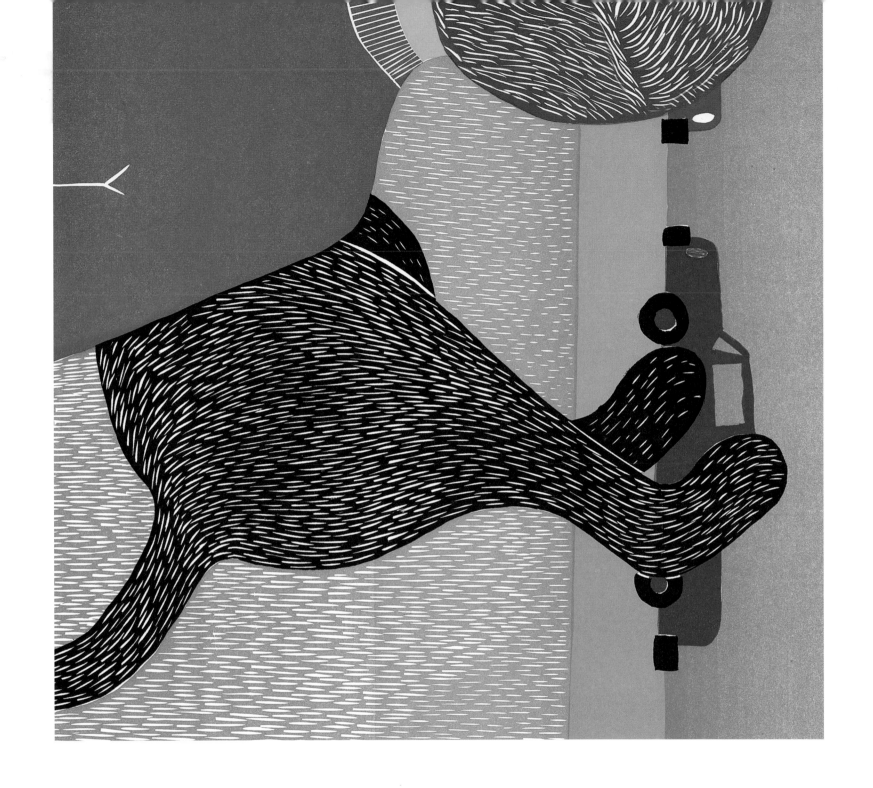

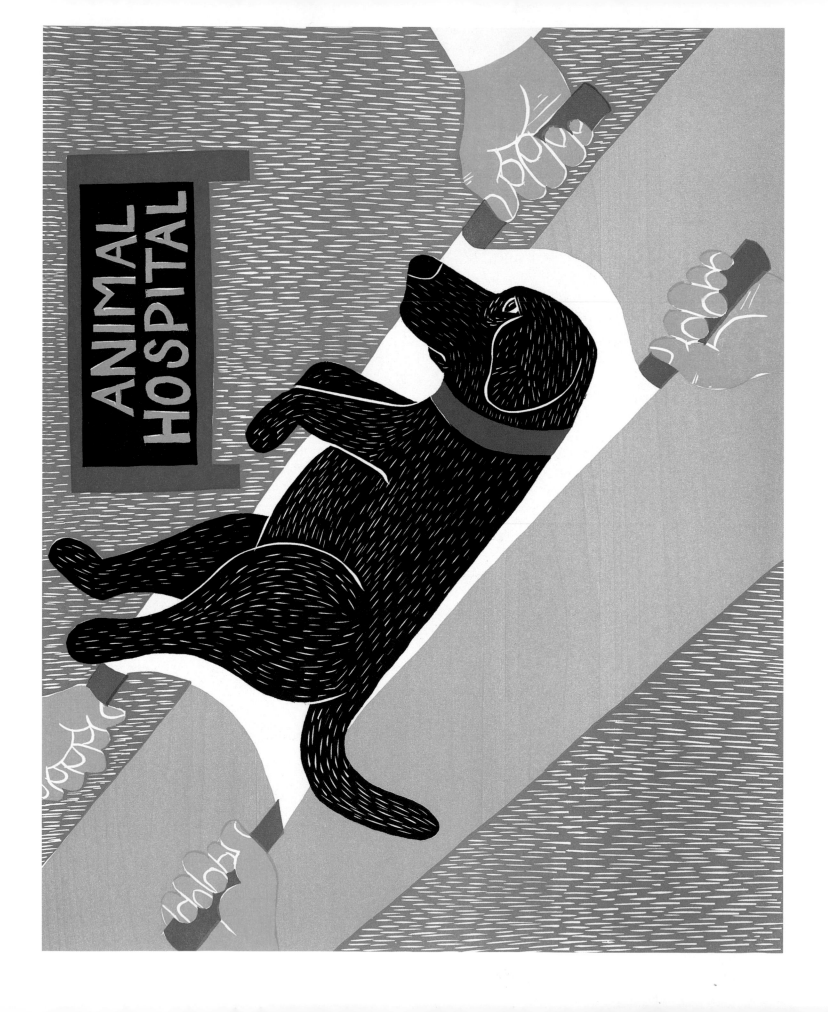

I am rushed right in.

I do not even have to wait!

"Do not worry, Sally, the doctor will be with you soon." The nurse explains that "vet" is short for doctor of veterinary medicine.

That means doctor of cats and rats,
dogs and frogs, parrots and ferrets,
snakes and turtles, and even goldfish, too!

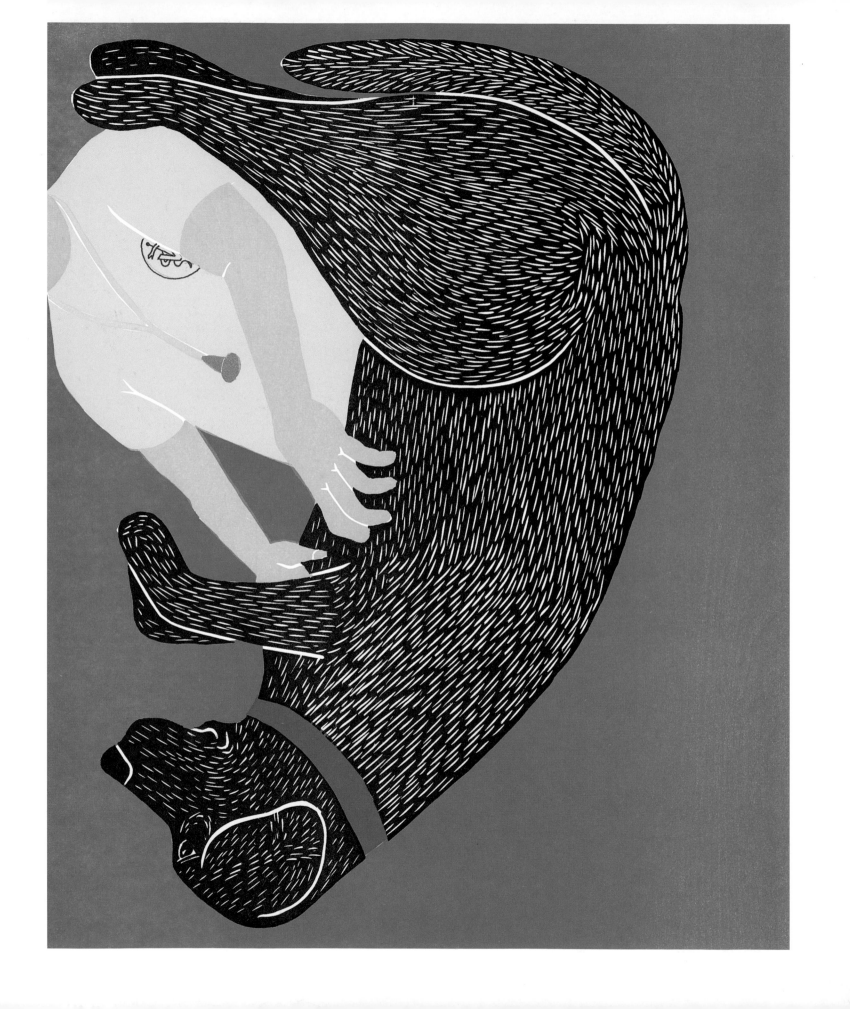

The vet examines me from nose to tail.
"Sally, you will need an X ray."

Will it hurt? I hear a click, and that is it.
"Lucky you! No broken bones," the vet tells me.

The vet looks in my eyes.

The vet looks down my throat.

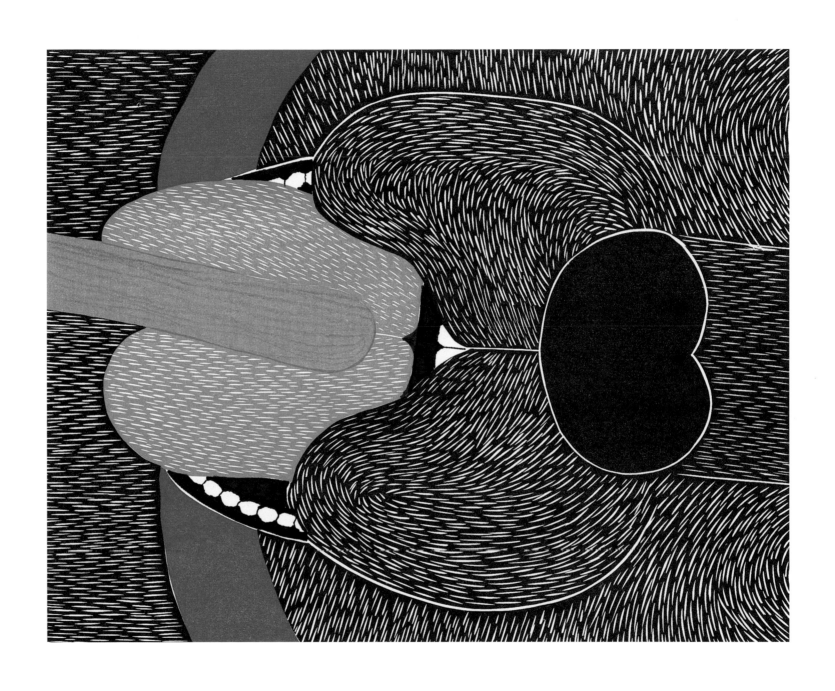

The vet listens to me breathe
and then listens to my heart.
"Sally, you will need a shot."

Will it hurt? "Just close your eyes and think a happy thought."

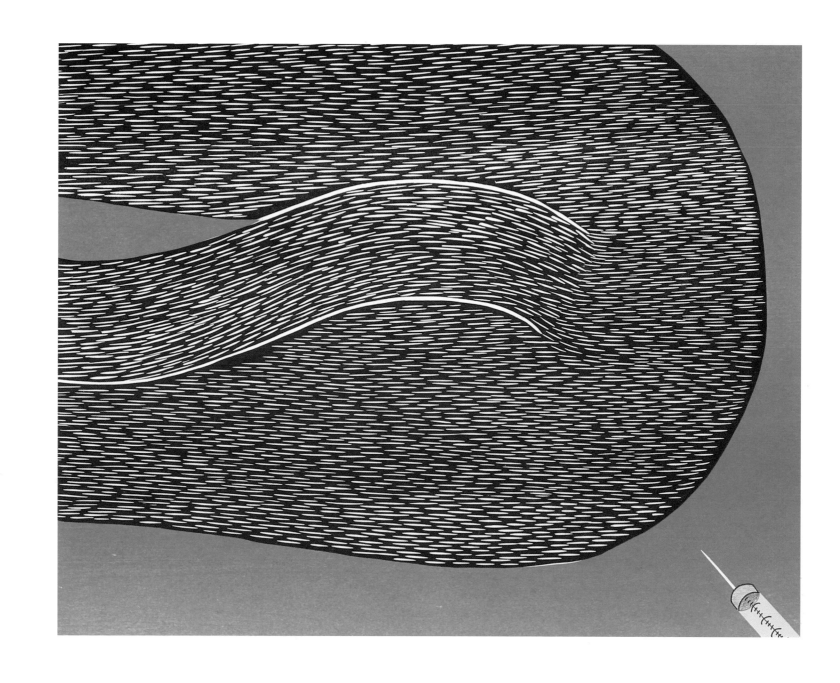

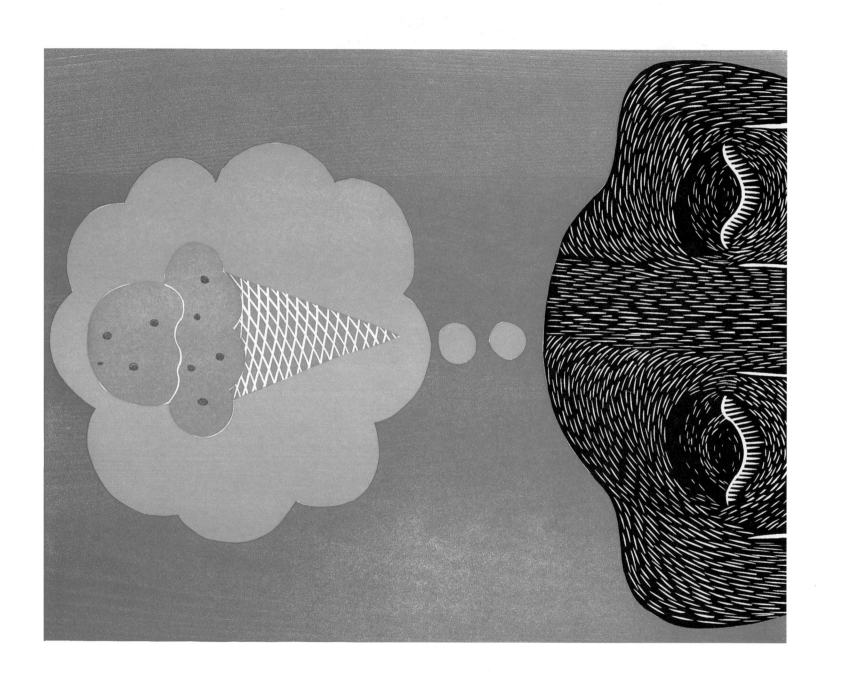

It really works! I hardly feel a thing.

"If you get lots of rest and take your medicine, you will be just fine."

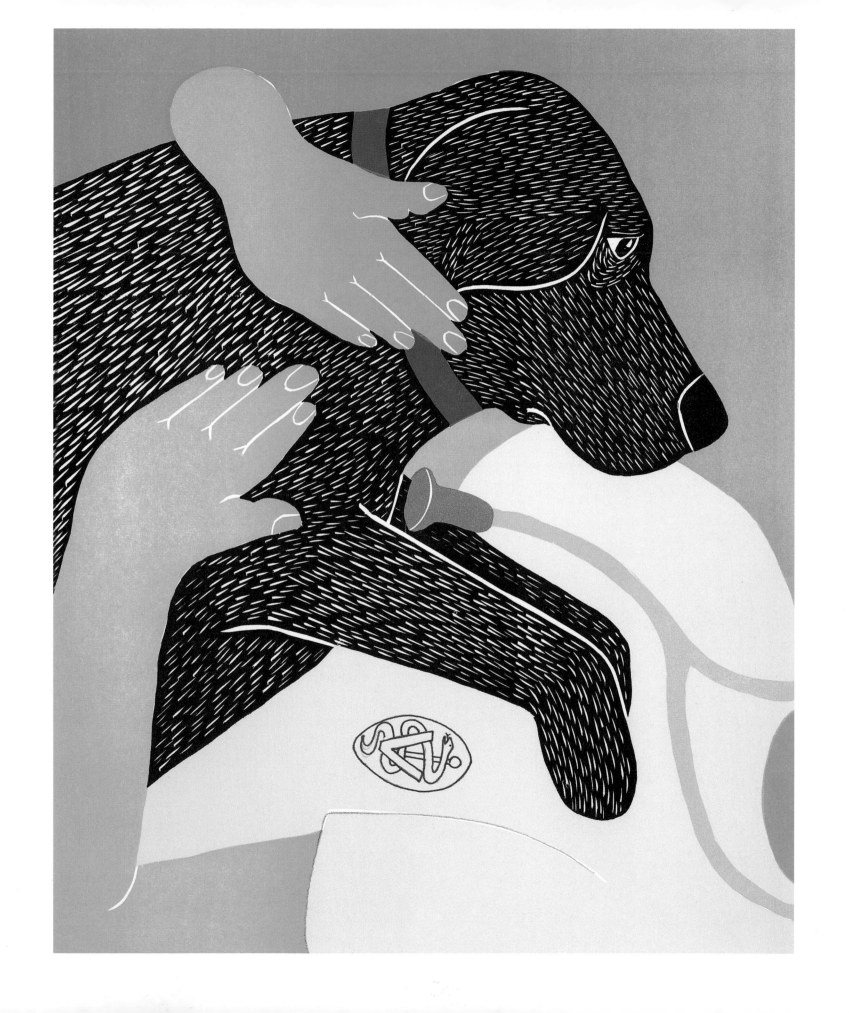

I am feeling so much better. I cannot wait to get home and tell Bingo all about my visit to the vet.

I tell Bingo about my X ray and about my shot, and what the vet taught me . . .

just close your eyes and think a happy thought!

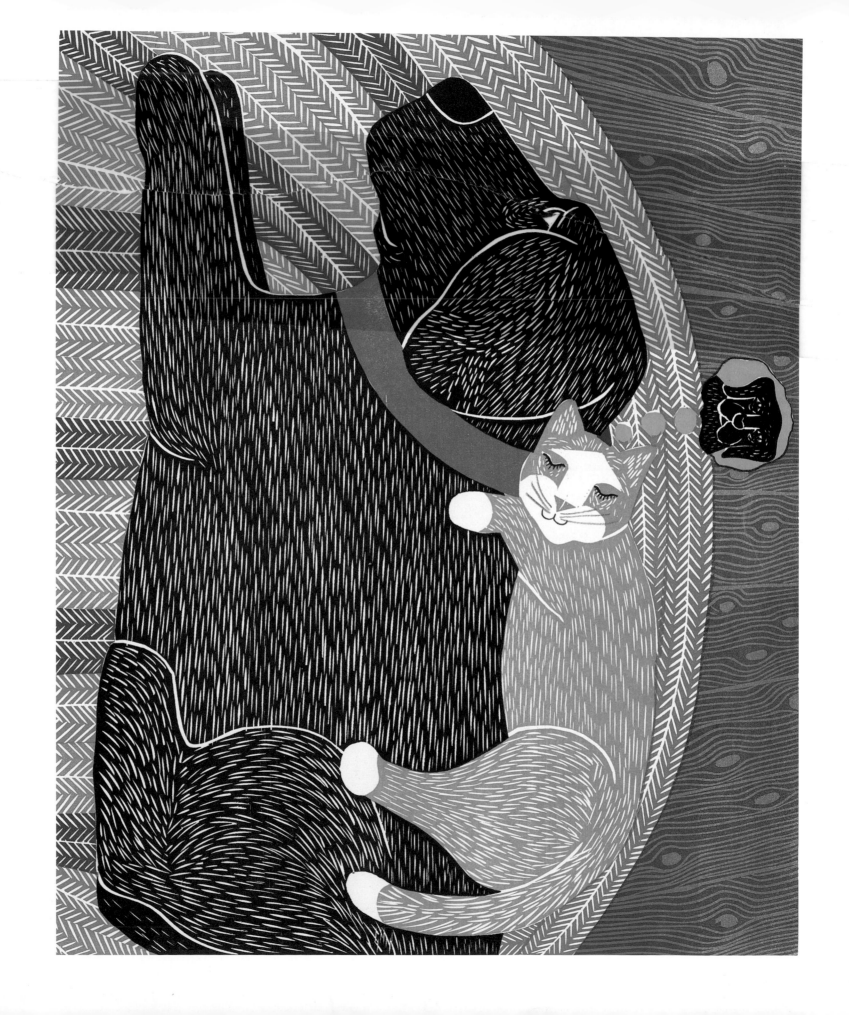